MATT AN

YUCK'S ROBOTIC BUTT BLAST

AND

YUCK'S WILD WEEKEND

Illustrated by Nigel Baines

A Paula Wiseman Book

Simon & Schuster Books for Young Readers
New York   London   Toronto   Sydney   New Delhi

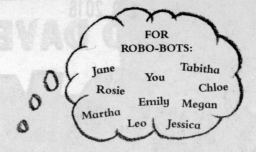

FOR
ROBO-BOTS:

Jane
Rosie
Martha
You
Emily
Leo
Tabitha
Chloe
Megan
Jessica

SIMON & SCHUSTER BOOKS FOR YOUNG READERS
An imprint of Simon & Schuster Children's Publishing Division
1230 Avenue of the Americas, New York, New York 10020
This book is a work of fiction. Any references to historical events, real people,
or real places are used fictitiously. Other names, characters, places, and events are products
of the author's imagination, and any resemblance to actual events or places
or persons, living or dead, is entirely coincidental.
Text copyright © 2009 by Matthew Morgan and David Sinden
Illustrations copyright © 2009 by Nigel Baines
Originally published in 2009 in Great Britain by Simon & Schuster UK, Ltd.
All rights reserved, including the right of reproduction in whole or in part in any form.
SIMON & SCHUSTER BOOKS FOR YOUNG READERS is a trademark of Simon & Schuster, Inc.
For information about special discounts for bulk purchases, please contact Simon & Schuster
Special Sales at 1-866-506-1949 or business@simonandschuster.com.
The Simon & Schuster Speakers Bureau can bring authors to your live event. For more
information or to book an event, contact the Simon & Schuster Speakers Bureau
at 1-866-248-3049 or visit our website at www.simonspeakers.com.
Also available in a Simon & Schuster Books for Young Readers hardcover edition
The text for this book is set in Bembo Std.
The illustrations for this book are rendered in pencil and ink.
Manufactured in the United States of America
0713 OFF
2 4 6 8 10 9 7 5 3
The Library of Congress has cataloged the hardcover edition as follows:
Morgan, Matthew, author.
[Short stories. Selections]
Yuck's robotic butt blast ; and Yuck's wild weekend / by Matt and Dave ;
illustrated by Nigel Baines.
pages cm. — (Yuck)
"A Paula Wiseman Book."
"Originally published in Great Britain in 2009 by Simon & Schuster UK Ltd"—Copyright page.
Summary: A naughty boy annoys his sister with his revolting inventions
and shenanigans on a camping trip.
ISBN 978-1-4424-8308-8 (hardcover) — ISBN 978-1-4424-8309-5 (pbk.) —
ISBN 978-1-4424-8310-1 (eBook)
[1. Behavior—Fiction. 2. Inventions—Fiction. 3. Camping—Fiction. 4. Brothers and sisters—
Fiction. 5. Humorous stories.] I. Sinden, David, author.
II. Baines, Nigel, illustrator. III. Morgan, Matthew. Yuck's robotic butt blast.
IV. Morgan, Matthew. Yuck's wild weekend. V. Title.
PZ7.M8254Yv 2013
[Fic]—dc23
2013006058
yuckweb.com

CAUTION:
YUCKY FUN INSIDE!

YUCK'S ROBOTIC BUTT BLAST

Yuck dangled a long piece of string from his bedroom window to the yard below. The string was covered with sticky red strawberry jam.

He watched excitedly as ants began crawling up the string, eating the jam. They crawled in a line, one after the other, all the way up to a jar on Yuck's windowsill.

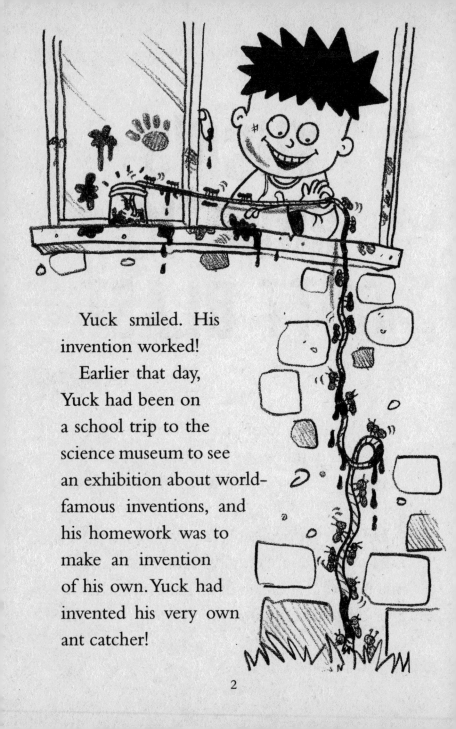

Yuck smiled. His invention worked!

Earlier that day, Yuck had been on a school trip to the science museum to see an exhibition about world-famous inventions, and his homework was to make an invention of his own. Yuck had invented his very own ant catcher!

He glanced down and saw his sister, Polly Princess, step into the yard. Attached to her shoes were two paper plates on drinking straws.

"Why are you wearing those?" Yuck called to her.

Polly looked up. "They're my invention," she told him. "They're umbrellas that keep my shoes dry in the rain. I call them shumbrellas."

"DUMBrellas, more like," Yuck said, giggling. "What a silly invention."

Polly scowled at Yuck. "You're just jealous because my invention's better than yours." She looked at the piece of string dangling from Yuck's window. "What's this for, anyway?" she asked, tugging it.

"Hey, hands off my ant catcher!"

"Aaargh!" Polly cried as ants showered down onto her. She shook her head and pulled at her hair trying to get them out. "I'm telling on you!"

She stormed indoors and a moment later Mom stepped out.

"Yuck, come downstairs at once!" Mom called.

"But, Mom—"

"No buts, Yuck.

Come down NOW!"

Yuck went downstairs to the kitchen and found Mom picking ants from Polly's hair. "Yuck, why did you throw ants on your sister?" Mom asked.

"I didn't," Yuck told her. "She did it herself. She was trying to ruin my invention."

Polly glared at Yuck. "An ant catcher's not a proper invention," she said. "It's disgusting."

"Polly's right, Yuck," Mom told him. "You'll have to invent something else."

While Mom finished picking the ants from Polly's hair, Yuck sneaked to the kitchen cupboard and took out a packet of chocolate cake mix. He headed back upstairs and set to work on another yucky inven-tion.

Using his baseball cap as a mixing bowl, Yuck shook in the chocolate cake mix, then fetched a tube of glue from his model-making box. He squeezed the glue into the hat and stirred it with the cake mix, making a sticky brown goo. *Perfect,* Yuck thought. He was inventing the world's stickiest fake dog poo!

He scooped out a handful, then stepped to his window. Polly Princess was back in the yard watering her shumbrellas with a watering can, testing to see if they worked. Yuck threw the dog poo onto the yard path behind her. "I bet it's difficult to walk in those," he called down.

Polly turned around. "It's easy." She walked down the path and stepped straight into the dog poo. "Uurgh!"

Polly tried to lift her foot but it was stuck. "Help! My shoe! My shoe's stuck in poo!"

Mom came running out of the back door. "What's the matter, Polly?"

"Sticky dog poo!" Polly shrieked.

"Dog poo?" Mom asked, confused. "But we haven't got a dog."

Mom glanced at Yuck's window as he ducked back into his room giggling.

Rockits! Yuck thought. *Inventions are fun!*

Yuck sneaked into Polly's room and bor-
rowed her Bubble Fun Bubble Maker from
her toy box. It was time for another yucky
invention. He put the Bubble Maker on his
bedroom floor and opened its lid where the
bubble mixture went. He filled
it with yucky ingredients:
half a glass of curdled
milk, a rotten
banana, and a lump
of moldy cheese
from an old sand-
wich. Then he took
off his smelly socks
and stuffed
those in
too, along
with a pair of dirty
underpants.
Yuck flicked
the switch on the
Bubble Maker and
it began rumbling

as bubbles started coming out. He was inventing a stink machine!

At that moment, his door burst open and Polly hopped in wearing only one shoe. "YOU put that sticky poo on the path, didn't you?" she said.

"Polly, can't you see I'm busy inventing?" Yuck told her. Polly saw bubbles floating around Yuck's room. She saw her Bubble Maker on the floor. "Hey, that's mine!"

"I've turned it into a stink machine. Do you like it?"

A bubble burst in Polly's face. "PHWOAR!" she cried, pinching her nose. It stank of moldy cheese. More bubbles burst around her, each letting off a different stink: curdled milk . . . smelly socks . . . rotten banana . . . dirty underpants . . .

"Mom!" Polly called. "Yuck's being disgusting again!"

Mom came running upstairs to Yuck's room and saw the bubbles bursting. She saw the baseball cap loaded with sticky dog poo, and the jam jar full of ants on his windowsill. "Yuck, get rid of these revolting inventions right now!" she yelled.

"But, Mom, they're for my homework," Yuck told her.

"These aren't proper inventions," Polly said, choking on a big bubble that stank of underpants. "They're gross."

"Polly's right, Yuck," Mom said. "You will not invent anything else yucky!"

Mom and Polly left Yuck's room and went downstairs coughing.

Yuck decided that when he was EMPEROR OF EVERYTHING, he'd invent all kinds of yucky things: slime-squirting spy planes, burp-blasting tanks, and even a sewage submarine.

If Polly tried to stop him, his inventions would launch an ATTACK!

Yuck stashed his yucky inventions under his bed, then tried to think what else he could make. He remembered the inventions at the science museum: the radio . . . the electric lightbulb . . . the television . . . the computer . . . the robot . . . Suddenly, Yuck's eyes lit up with excitement! *A ROBOT!* he thought. He could have LOTS of fun with a robot! If only he knew how to make one. . . .

That night, Yuck was lying in bed, thinking how he could invent a robot, when he had a brilliant idea. While everyone was asleep, he crept downstairs to the yard and searched in Dad's shed. He found some old cardboard boxes and carried them indoors. From the hall cupboard, he fetched some shiny colored wrapping paper, a roll of tape, and a stack of gift labels. He wrapped the boxes in the shiny paper and stuck a label with a handwritten message to each. Finally, he placed them outside the front door to make it look like they'd been delivered by the mailman.

In the morning, he woke up hearing Mom calling up the stairs. "Yuck, there are some packages here for you!"

Yuck quickly dressed and raced down to see. "Packages? I wonder who they could be from?" he said innocently.

Polly came downstairs to see what was happening. "Why does Yuck have packages?" she asked.

On the front doorstep were the boxes in shiny paper, just as he'd left them the night before.

Polly pushed past him and snatched one of them. She read its label: "To Professor Yuck, from NASA Space Research. **TOP SECRET.**"

She looked at Yuck. "It says 'Professor.' You're not a professor."

She checked the labels on the other packages.

"To Professor Yuck, from Robotico Research. **TOP SECRET.**

"To Professor Yuck, from Inventors, Inc. **TOP SECRET.**"

Yuck smiled. "Oh, these must be the top-secret scientific parts I've been waiting for."

"Top-secret scientific parts?"

"For my new invention."

"What invention?" Polly asked.

"A robot!" Yuck told her. "I'm inventing a walking, talking, remote-controlled robot."

"Hey, that's not fair," Polly said jealously. She watched as Yuck picked up the packages, balancing them one on top of the other, and stepped out of the door

"I'll see you at school," he said, smiling. But for his robot plan to work, Yuck would need a friend to help him. And he knew just the person to ask.

At the school gates, Yuck saw his friend Little Eric shaking people's hands as they arrived. Each person yelped and leaped into the air.

"How did you do that?" Yuck asked.

Little Eric showed Yuck a metal buzzer in his hand.

"Is that your invention?"

"It's a Buzz-o-laff," Little Eric whispered. "I got it free with *Klunk* magazine." He stared up at Yuck's stack of packages. "What are you doing with those?"

"I'm inventing a robot," Yuck told him. "Come on. You can help."

They needed a place where no one would see them, so they sneaked to the school bathroom. Yuck put the packages down.

"What's in them?" Little Eric asked.

"Nothing." Yuck giggled. "Watch this."

Yuck tore a hole in either end of one of the packages and slid it onto Little Eric's arm. Then he made holes in another package and slid it onto Little Eric's leg. One after the other, Yuck slid all the packages onto Little Eric, com-pletely covering his body. He put the last pack-age over Little Eric's head. With a felt-tipped pen he drew on but-tons, dials, nuts, and bolts. He drew on a robot mouth and robot ears, then pulled off the gift labels

and tore a small slit for Little Eric to see through. Finally, he fetched ten toilet-paper tubes and slid them onto Little Eric's fingers. "Finished," he said.

Little Eric stepped out of the stall and looked in the mirror. "Brilliant!" he said. He looked just like a robot!

"Try talking like a robot," Yuck told him.

"**BLEEP, BLIP, BLOOP**," Little Eric replied, speaking in a robot voice.

"Perfect," Yuck said. From his bag, he took a remote control. It was the one for the TV at home. "I'll pretend to control you with this." Yuck pointed the remote control at Little Eric and pressed a button. Little Eric started walking like a robot.

"Don't let anyone know it's you," Yuck said, and they headed to class.

Yuck peered through the classroom door and saw Mrs. Wagon the Dragon taking attendance. Everyone was sitting at their desks with their inventions. Schoolie Julie had invented a fan to stop ice cream melting in the sun. Fartin' Martin and Tom Butts had invented rocket pants to help them run faster. Kate the Skate had invented a bendy skateboard for skating around corners.

As Yuck crept in, the Dragon grabbed him. "You're late, Yuck!"

"Sorry, Mrs. Wagon, I've been finishing my invention," Yuck said.

"Oh, yes? And what have you invented?" the Dragon asked.

"A robot," Yuck told her.

The Dragon raised her glasses and stared at Yuck in astonishment. "A robot?"

"That's right." Yuck pointed his remote control toward the door. He pressed a button and in stepped Little Eric dressed in the robot costume.

The class gasped. "Wow! A real robot!"

"**BLEEP, BLIP, BLOOP,**" the robot said, marching toward the Dragon.

"It's a walking, talking, remote-controlled robot," Yuck explained.

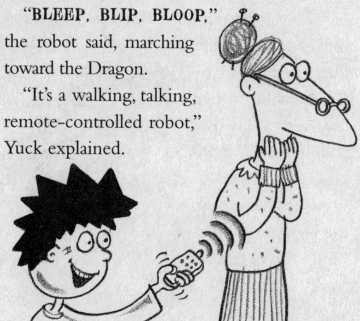

"How remarkable!" the Dragon said, inspecting it. "You invented this all by yourself?"

The robot held out its hand to the Dragon. "**BLOOP, BLEEP, BLIP**. Pleased to meet you," it said.

As the Dragon shook the robot's hand, she leaped into the air. "Aaaargh!" she yelped.

"Oh dear. You must have gotten an electric shock," Yuck told her.

The robot was giggling. Little Eric still had the Buzz-o-laff strapped to his hand.

Yuck pointed his

Aaaargh!

remote control and directed the robot to an empty seat at the back of the class. He sat beside it. "We fooled her," he whispered.

The Dragon's hair was standing on end from the Buzz-o-laff. She looked at the attendance sheet. "Does anyone know where Little Eric is today?" she asked.

Megan the Mouth put her hand up. "He was at the school gates this morning, Mrs. Wagon."

The robot put its hand up. "**BLEEP, BLIP, BLOOP**. He went home feeling ill," it said.

The Dragon looked at the robot, surprised to hear it answer.

Yuck quickly put his hand up. "Little Eric's definitely not here, Mrs. Wagon," he said.

The Dragon marked Little Eric as absent. "Well, I'm delighted to announce that Mrs. Appliance from the science museum will be coming to school tomorrow to see your inventions. What's more, for the best invention in school, she'll be awarding two tickets to Space World."

"Space World! Fantastic!" everyone said.

Space World was a theme park with space rockets, space food, and intergalactic rides. Yuck had always wanted to go there.

"I suggest you spend today making sure your inventions are in tip-top working order," the Dragon continued. She started walking among the desks, seeing what everyone had invented.

Inside the robot costume Little Eric's nose was twitching. The box on his head was dusty. "ATCHOO!"

Ben Bongo turned around from the desk in front. "Did your robot just sneeze?" he asked Yuck.

Snot was leaking from the box on Little Eric's head. Yuck wiped it off and rubbed it between his fingers. "It's robot oil," he said.

Frank the Tank turned around to see. "Why's your robot wearing glasses?" he asked.

"Those aren't glasses, they're laser goggles," Yuck said.

"Laser goggles?"

Yuck pointed to a red button on the remote control. "If I press this button, its eyes fire laser beams—exterminator beams!"

Frank the Tank stared in awe at the robot. "How did you manage to build it?"

Yuck smiled. "It's easy when you're a brilliant inventor like me."

At break time, Yuck took his robot to the playground to have some fun. He pointed the control and pressed a button. The robot spun around. He pressed another button and the robot jumped up and down. He pressed another button and the robot did a robot dance. Soon a crowd had gathered to watch. Polly Princess and her friend Juicy Lucy pushed to the front.

"Polly, how did Yuck invent a robot?" Juicy Lucy whispered, seeing the robot do a blip-bleep boogie.

"He should be disqualified," Polly replied. "He had top-secret scientific parts delivered this morning." She dashed to Yuck and snatched the remote control from his hand.

"Hey, give that back!" Yuck said.

Polly pressed a button trying to send the robot into the school pond. But the robot kept dancing. "It's broken," she said, shaking the control. She pressed all the buttons, trying to make the robot short-circuit.

"Not the red one!" Frank the Tank called.

The robot stopped dancing and began marching toward Polly. "Prepare laser beams. **BLEEP**," it said.

"Run, Polly! It's got exterminator beams!" Frank the Tank warned her.

"Exterminator beams?"

The robot stared straight at her. "**BLEEP**, **BLOOP**, **BLIP**! Exterminate Polly! Exterminate Polly!"

Polly began quivering.

"They melt you like butter," Yuck said.

Polly dropped the remote control and fled across the playground. Mr. Reaper, the principal, came out to see what the noise was and Polly ran straight into him, knocking him to the ground.

"Watch where you're going!" the Reaper yelled.

"But, Mr. Reaper, a robot's after me!" Polly said.

The Reaper stood up, brushing off his pants. "A robot? What robot?" He looked across the playground and saw the robot standing beside Yuck. He came walking over. "Where did this robot come from, Yuck?" he asked.

"I invented it, Mr. Reaper," Yuck replied.

"How remarkable! You invented a robot all by yourself?"

"Yes, sir. It's a walking, talking, remote-controlled robot. Let me show you." Yuck pressed a button on the remote control and the robot headed off back into school. Yuck ran after it, leaving the Reaper amazed.

Yuck whispered to Little Eric: "We've fooled them all. Space World, here we come!"

At lunchtime, Yuck and his robot sat in the school cafeteria with plates of sausages, beans, and french fries. Little Eric found it difficult to hold a fork with his toilet-paper-tube fingers, and the robot head had no hole for its mouth.

"Let me help you," Yuck said, making a small tear in the cardboard. He pushed a sausage through and Little Eric giggled.

"That went up my nose!"

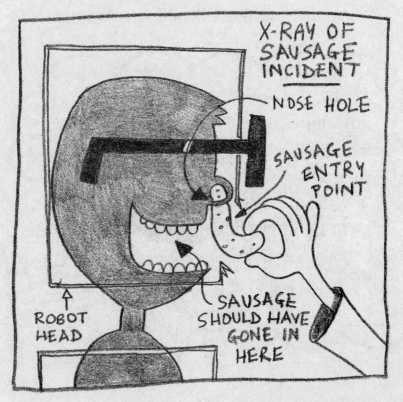

X-RAY OF SAUSAGE INCIDENT

NOSE HOLE

SAUSAGE ENTRY POINT

ROBOT HEAD

SAUSAGE SHOULD HAVE GONE IN HERE

From a nearby table, Polly and Lucy were watching.

"Robots don't eat sausages," Lucy whispered.

They watched as the robot tried to eat beans. Tomato sauce dribbled down its chin, then it let out a *BURP!*

"Robots don't burp, either," Polly replied. "Yuck's up to something. I'm sure of it."

All through lunchtime, they spied on Yuck and his robot. On the playground, they heard Yuck telling the robot a joke.

"What do robots eat for dinner?"

"**BLIP, BLEEP, BLOOP**. I don't know. What do robots eat for dinner?"

"Microchips!"

Yuck and the robot both laughed.

"Robots don't laugh," Polly whispered.

Polly and Lucy crouched in the bushes,

watching Yuck and the robot play soccer. The robot cheered when it scored: "Goal!"

"Robots don't cheer, either," Lucy whispered.

A while later, Polly and Lucy saw Yuck and his robot go into the boys' room.

"Robots definitely don't go to the bathroom!" Polly said.

Polly and Lucy sneaked in after them. They saw Yuck go into one stall and his robot go into another. They crept to the stall with the robot in it and peered under the door. The robot was sliding packages from its legs. Underneath, it was wearing pants!

"That's not a robot!" Polly said.

Polly barged through the door and saw the robot sitting on the toilet! She yanked its head and a box came off in her hands. "It's Little Eric!" Polly and Lucy gasped.

Little Eric pulled his pants up and leaped from the toilet. "Yuck, help!" he called.

"So this is what you've been up to!" Polly said. "Well, now the game's up!" She tore the boxes from Little Eric's arms and legs, ripping them to pieces.

Yuck burst into the stall. "Leave Little Eric alone!"

"Oh dear, Yuck," Polly said, smirking. "It looks like your robot's broken now."

Little Eric was picking up pieces of cardboard. Polly pushed past him. "Come on, Lucy. Let's go."

"Now what are we going to do?" Little Eric said to Yuck. "Without the robot, we'll never win the tickets to Space World."

That evening, Yuck decided he'd build a new robot costume. But when he looked in Dad's shed for more cardboard boxes, they were all gone. He found Dad in the living room watching television. "Dad, what happened to the cardboard boxes in your shed?"

"Your sister took them," Dad replied.

Yuck raced upstairs and opened Polly's bedroom door. There, standing by her bed, was a new robot! It was Polly, dressed in a brand-new robot costume of her own!

"Hey, what do you think you're doing?" Yuck asked.

Polly laughed. "**BLEEP, BLOOP, BLIP**. If you tell, I'll exterminate you." She took off her robot head and glared at him. "It's Lucy and me who'll be going to Space World now!"

That night, Yuck lay in bed thinking what to do. Tomorrow, Mrs. Appliance from the science museum would be coming to school. If he didn't find a way to stop Polly, she'd win the prize for best invention.

At that moment, Yuck smelled a stink wafting from under his bed. He leaned down and saw his yucky inventions: the jar of ants, the hat of sticky dog poo, and his stink machine. He had an idea!

Yuck hid the jar and the poo in his backpack, then carried the stink machine to Polly's room. She was snoring and her robot costume was lying on the floor. Yuck rummaged through it and opened one of the boxes. He placed the stink machine inside, then took a cardboard tube and attached it to the box like an exhaust pipe. Tomorrow, Polly would be in for a surprise. . . .

The next day at school, everyone gathered in the auditorium with their inventions. Polly was wearing her robot costume and Lucy was beside her holding a remote control.

"Yuck, why don't we tell the Reaper what they're up to?" Little Eric whispered.

"Because I've got a plan," Yuck replied. He opened his backpack and showed Little Eric the jar of ants and the hat full of sticky dog poo. Then they crept behind Polly, and Yuck  pointed to the back of her costume where the cardboard tube was poking from the robot's butt. Yuck whispered something to Little Eric and Little Eric giggled. They watched as Mrs. Appliance from the science museum came in with the Reaper.

Mrs. Appliance began inspecting each invention in turn. Schoolie Julie demonstrated her fan for cooling ice cream. But when she switched it on, the ice cream blew in her face.

Fartin' Martin and Tom Butts showed Mrs. Appliance their rocket pants for rocket-powered running. But when they turned on the gas, the pants blew up with a BANG!

Kate the Skate tried out her bendy skateboard for going around corners, but it spun around and around in circles, making her dizzy.

"I'm sorry about this," the Reaper said to Mrs. Appliance. "I'm sure some-one will have invented something that works."

Mrs. Appliance inspected the inventions, but they were all useless. Finally she reached Juicy Lucy and her robot. "How remarkable," Mrs. Appliance said. "A robot! Did you make this yourself?"

"I invented it with my friend Polly," Juicy Lucy explained.

The Reaper looked down at Lucy. "And

where is Polly today?" he asked.

"She's not at school," Lucy lied. "I think she's sick." Lucy pressed a button on the remote control. Inside the costume, Polly moved her arm and the robot waved.

"How ingenious!" Mrs. Appliance said.

Juicy Lucy pressed another button and the robot took a step forward.

"How incredible!" Mrs. Appliance said.

Lucy pressed another button and the robot spoke: "**BLIP, BLEEP, BLOOP**. Hello."

"Genius! A walking, talking, remote-controlled robot!" Mrs. Appliance said. "This is by far the best invention in the school."

Yuck stepped behind the robot and sneakily reached into the box on its butt. He flicked the switch on his stink machine inside, and the robot's butt started rumbling. A bubble leaked from the cardboard tube and burst, letting off a stinky gas.

"Phwoargh!" Mrs. Appliance said. "What's that awful smell?"

"It stinks!" the Reaper added, waving his arms to clear the air.

Yuck peered around from behind the robot. "I think the robot's malfunctioning," he said.

Little Eric pointed to the robot's butt. More bubbles were coming out of it. "It seems to be farting!"

Yuck and Little Eric giggled as bubbles floated from the robot's butt and burst in the air.

"Phwoargh! What a stink!" Lucy said. The bubbles smelled like dirty underpants.

While everyone was coughing and choking, Yuck reached into his bag and grabbed his jar of ants. Sneakily, he poured them into the box at the back of the robot.

The robot started twitching. "Eek, **BLEEP**, ooo!" it said. It began hopping from one leg to the other. Inside the robot costume, ants were crawling up and down Polly's legs. They were biting her. "**BLIP**, argh! **BLOOP**, ouch!"

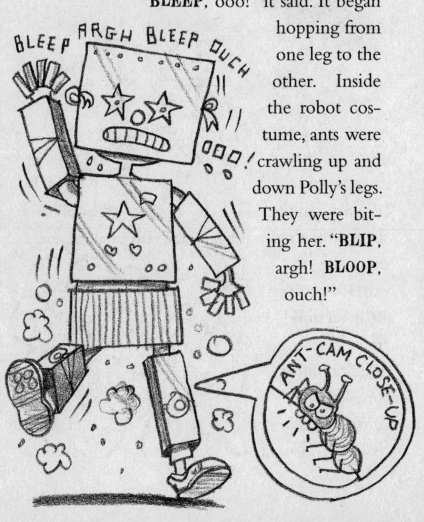

"Why is this robot behaving so oddly?" Mrs. Appliance asked Lucy.

"I have no idea," Lucy replied.

The robot was hopping and screaming. "Ow! **BLOOP!** Argh!"

It started running through the auditorium, barging past the other children, knocking into their inventions. Its butt was firing out bubbles: streams of them, one after the other, bursting with terrible smells.

"Stop that robot!" the Reaper cried.

All the children were pinching their noses. "It stinks!"

Bubbles were bursting everywhere. They smelled of curdled milk, smelly socks, rotten banana, moldy cheese, and dirty underpants.

"*PHWOAR!*" everyone cried.

"Lucy, make it stop!" the Reaper ordered.

"But I can't!" Lucy said, chasing the robot.

She was pointing the remote control, frantically pressing buttons. "Stop!" she cried. "Stop!"

But the robot was out of control.

Yuck stepped beside Mrs. Appliance. "Leave this to me!" he said. From his bag, he took out a lump of sticky brown goo.

"What's that?" Mrs. Appliance asked him.

"This is one of my inventions," Yuck replied. "It's the world's stickiest dog poo." He threw the poo across the auditorium and it splatted in the robot's path.

The robot stepped in the poo and its foot stuck to the floor. "**BLEEEEP!** I'm stuck!" it cried.

"What a brilliant invention," Mrs. Appliance said to Yuck.

She ran to the robot, which was now coughing and struggling. "Get me out of here! Get me out of here!" it shouted.

"This isn't a real robot!" the Reaper said, walking toward it. "There's someone in here!" The Reaper yanked off the robot's head. . . .

"Polly!" the Reaper said angrily. "What a cheater! You and Lucy are in BIG TROUBLE."

Polly's face was crawling with ants. "*HELP!*" she screamed. "*GET THEM OFF ME!*"

Yuck stepped forward. "Leave this to me," he said. From his bag he took out a jam jar and a length of string covered in jam. He laid the string on the ground and the ants began crawling along it, away from Polly, back toward the jar.

Mrs. Appliance stared in astonishment as Yuck gathered all the ants back up. "How brilliant!" she exclaimed.

"This is my ant catcher," Yuck told her. "It's another of my inventions."

"Help me!" Polly coughed. "Help me!" She was surrounded by bursting bubbles, choking on the stench. The robot's butt was still farting. "Make it stop!"

"Leave this to me," Yuck said again. He slid the cardboard box from the robot's butt, then reached in and turned off the stink machine. The bubbles stopped.

"How did you do that?" Mrs. Appliance asked.

"This is my invention too," Yuck told her.

Mrs. Appliance stared in astonishment at the box with the cardboard tube poking from it. "This is incredible!" she said. "I've never seen anything like it. Do you realize what you've invented? This is the world's first robotic butt!"

She took two tickets from her pocket and gave them to Yuck. "Here you are. I award you the prize for the best invention in the school: two tickets to Space World."

Yuck smiled and handed a ticket to Little Eric. "Space World, here we come!"

YUCK'S WILD WEEKEND

A hairy hand with long nails reached over Yuck's shoulder. He glanced around. Little Eric was wearing his Hairy-Bear Beast Glove, making the sign of THE CLAW.

"*GRRRR* . . . Are we ready to explore the wild?" Little Eric asked.

Yuck held his hand up, returning the secret sign. "*GRRRR* . . . The equipment is prepared."

On Yuck's bed was a backpack and a pile of survival equipment: a tent, sleeping bags, a flashlight, a compass, a catapult, snowshoes, a fishing rod, a net, and a rope.

"What about the food rations?" Little Eric asked.

By Yuck's feet lay two empty Chocoblock wrappers. "We've eaten them," he said. "We'll just have to survive on what we can find." He was holding a book called *How to Survive in*

the Wild. It was written by Bushtucker Bill and was full of ways to survive in wild places: in a jungle, on a mountain, in the desert, and even in a snowstorm.

Yuck and Little Eric loaded the equipment into the backpack, then put on hats that they'd camouflaged with lettuce leaves. They grabbed the fishing rod, net, and rope, and ran downstairs.

Mom was in the kitchen clearing the plates from lunch. "So that's where my lettuce went," she said, seeing Yuck and Little Eric's hats as they crept past. "You're supposed to eat your salad, Yuck, not wear it."

"But this is camouflage, Mom," Yuck told her. "We're off to the wild!"

Yuck opened the back door and ran outside.

"Be good," Mom called.

Yuck and Little Eric were off on a wild weekend! They were going camping in the backyard. They raced across the lawn and stopped under a tall tree.

Yuck placed the backpack on the ground. "We'll pitch our tent here," he said.

But just then, Yuck's sister, Polly Princess, called from the house, "Oh, no, you won't!" She came running across the yard toward them. She was wearing a backpack too! Little Eric's sister, Juicy Lucy, was with her, carrying a yellow blanket.

Polly raced to Yuck. "What do you think you're doing?" she asked.

"You know what we're doing. We're camping in the yard," Yuck told her.

"Oh, no, you're not. Lucy and I are

camping in the yard this weekend."

"But you said you were going to the movies," Yuck replied.

Polly grinned. "We've changed our minds."

"You won't like it in the wild," Yuck told Polly. "There are dangerous animals and sinking swamps and—"

"You need special survival equipment," Little Eric added. He was holding the net and rope and fishing rod.

"Nonsense," Polly said. She snatched Yuck's backpack and threw it in the bushes.

"Hey, why did you do that?"

Dad looked over from his vegetable patch. "Play nicely," he called. "There's plenty of room for all of you."

Polly pushed Yuck out of the way and started unpacking her kit: sunscreen . . . sunglasses . . . a radio . . . magazines . . .

Lucy laid the yellow blanket on the ground. "Now go away. We were here first," she sneered.

"Come on, Eric. We'll find somewhere better to camp," Yuck said, pulling his backpack from the bushes. He headed to the other side of the yard by the fence.

"Why do they always have to ruin everything?" Little Eric said. "They're only camping because we are."

Yuck decided that when he was EMPEROR OF EVERYTHING, he'd live in a big tent in a wild forest full of beasts. If Polly tried to come camping, he'd send the beasts to GOBBLE HER UP.

As Yuck and Little Eric started putting their tent up, a breeze wafted across the yard toward Polly and Lucy.

"Phwoar!" Polly called. "Your tent stinks!"

Yuck's tent was still damp from the last time he'd been camping and had packed it away wet with rain. It had mold and fungus growing on it and smelled like a compost heap.

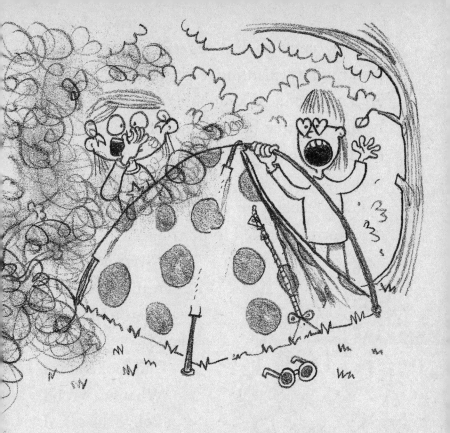

Yuck saw Polly pinching her nose. "It serves you right for stealing our place," he called to her. Polly and Lucy were putting their tent up under the tree. It was pink with purple spots.

"Their tent looks like it's got measles," Little Eric said, giggling.

"I've got an idea," Yuck whispered. "Watch this."

Yuck crept to the vegetable patch where Dad was busy planting seeds. Sneakily, he gathered a handful of long, juicy worms, then ran behind the tree by Polly and Lucy's tent. He reached out, laying the worms among their tent stakes.

Polly reached for a stake. "Eeek!" she cried as a worm wriggled in her fingers.

"Urrgh!" Lucy screamed, seeing it wrap around Polly's hand.

Dad looked over. "What's wrong, Polly?" he called.

"It's revolting!" Polly shrieked. "There are worms in our tent stakes!"

Yuck was giggling.

As he raced back to Little Eric, Polly shouted, "Just you wait, Yuck! I'll get you for this!"

When their camp was ready, Yuck and Little Eric set off to explore the wild. They streaked mud on their faces and lay on their stomachs, crawling across the lawn, pretending they were on a jungle safari.

"Keep your eyes peeled," Yuck whispered. "There's danger in the jungle, remember."

Little Eric was following a trail of slime. "Look, there's a jungle slime beast!" he said, pointing to a slug.

"And there's a man-eating spider!" Yuck said, pointing to a spider's web on a bush. A hairy garden spider was crawling across it.

Just then, a tennis ball flew over and smacked Yuck on the head. "Ow!" He looked across the yard and saw Polly standing by her tent holding a tennis racket.

"Oops!" Polly called. "Did I accidentally hit you with my ball?"

"Leave us alone, Polly," Yuck called back. "We're exploring the jungle."

Polly was laughing at them. "Don't be silly. This isn't the jungle. It's the yard."

"And you both look stupid," Lucy added.

Polly and Lucy ducked inside their tent, sniggering.

"Look what they've done," Little Eric said. He pointed to the spider's web. Polly's ball had gone right through it and the spider was now hanging by a thread.

"Let's teach them a lesson," Yuck whispered. He cupped the spider in his hand, then sneaked across the yard and placed it at the entrance to Polly  and Lucy's tent. The spider crawled inside.

Little Eric ran over with a handful of slug slime and they hid behind the tree.

In the tent, Polly was whispering to Lucy, "They're not explorers. They're just naughty boys."

"I wish they'd go indoors," Lucy said. "Then we'd have the yard to ourselves."

Just then, Polly felt something crawling up her leg. It was scuttling up inside her pants.

"Aaargh!" she screamed, leaping from the tent.

Little Eric threw the slug slime onto the blanket and Polly slipped in it. "Urgh!"

Lucy poked her head out.
"Are you okay, Polly?"

Polly was sliding
on the slug slime.
"Something's crawl-
ing in my pants!"

Dad rushed
over. "What's
wrong, Polly?"

Polly was fran-
tically shaking her
leg. "Get it off me!"

A spider crawled out and Dad picked it up.
"It's just a friendly garden spider," he said. "It's
perfectly harmless, Polly." He carried it to the
bushes, then went back to his gardening.

Polly saw Yuck and Little Eric giggling by
the tree. "That was you two, wasn't it? I'll get
you back!"

Yuck and Little Eric quickly raced across
the yard. "That'll teach her to mess with
explorers." Little Eric said with a laugh.

They ducked into their tent and searched

among their survival equipment, preparing for another expedition. "Let's put on our snow-shoes and explore the Arctic," Yuck said.

From the backpack he pulled out two old tennis rackets and tied them to his sneakers. Little Eric tied two old table tennis paddles to his. They walked side by side across the lawn pretending they were tramping through deep snow.

"Which way to the North Pole?" Little Eric asked.

Yuck checked his compass. "That way," he said, pointing along the fence.

They pretended they were struggling through a snowy blizzard.

"It's c-c-cold here," Yuck said, his teeth chattering.

Little Eric pretended to shiver. "We have to k-keep g-going."

At that moment, a Frisbee flew over and whacked Little Eric on the head. He turned and saw Polly and Lucy giggling.

"Why are you wearing those things on your feet?" Lucy called.

"These are snowshoes," Little Eric called back. "We're exploring the Arctic."

Lucy laughed. "Don't be silly. This isn't the Arctic. It's the yard."

"And you both look stupid," Polly added.

Polly and Lucy were lying on their blanket trying to sunbathe.

Yuck whispered in Little Eric's ear. "Let's see how they deal with an arctic snowstorm."

Yuck and Little Eric took off their snow-shoes, then crept to the tree by Polly and Lucy's tent. They climbed up it and crawled along a branch. Yuck looked down through the leaves. He scratched his head, and Little Eric did the same.  Large flakes of white dandruff began falling down onto Polly and Lucy.

"Hey, it's snowing," Lucy said, confused.

Polly sat up. "It can't be. It's summertime."

Lucy poked her tongue out to catch a snowflake.

Polly looked up and saw Yuck and Little
Eric in the tree above, scratching their heads.
"Urgh, this isn't snow! It's dandruff!"

Lucy looked up. "That's revolting!" she said, spitting the dandruff from her mouth.

Yuck and Little Eric climbed down and raced across the yard. They dived into their tent, rolling around with laughter.

Yuck told Little Eric a joke: "What do snowmen eat for breakfast?"

"I don't know, what do snowmen eat for breakfast?"

"Snowflakes!"

Just then, their tent collapsed, covering them in a bundle of moldy cloth. "Hey, what's going on?" Little Eric asked.

They could hear footsteps outside. Little Eric fumbled for the zipper, then poked his head out. Polly and Lucy had untied their tent ropes.

"Oh dear, your tent's fallen down," Polly called, running back across the yard. "Perhaps you'd better go indoors."

Yuck and Little Eric crawled from the bundle of moldy material. "We'll get them back," Yuck whispered. "Watch this." He took off one of his socks. It was stripy and long. He poked a twig in its end to look like a forked tongue. "*HISSSSSSSSS*," he said. "Let's see how they handle THE SNAKE."

Yuck and Little Eric sneaked to Polly and Lucy's tent. They could hear music coming from inside. Polly had her radio on and Lucy was singing. Yuck poked his sock through the entrance. "*HISSSSSSSSS*."

Inside the tent, Polly tugged Lucy's arm.

"What's that sound?" she asked.

"*HISSSSSSSSS.*"

Lucy stopped singing. "It sounds like a—"

"AAARGH!" Polly shrieked, seeing a snake slithering into the tent, its tongue sticking out, hissing.

"*HISSSSSSSSSSSSSSSSS.*"

"Snake!" she cried.

"Help! It's going to bite us!" Lucy screamed. She picked up Polly's radio and whacked the snake on the head.

The radio smashed.

Just then, the tent's zipper opened. It was Dad. "What's going on in here?" he asked.

"A snake's trying to bite us," Lucy said.

Dad looked down. He pinched his nose. "Polly, Lucy, it's just a smelly sock."

"A sock?"

Yuck stepped out from behind the tree. "Oh, there it is," he said. "I've been looking every-where for that." Yuck grabbed the sock, then ran back with Little Eric. They dived into their tent, laughing.

From the side pocket of the backpack Yuck took out his book: *How to Survive in the Wild*. He flicked through the pages, looking at Bushtucker Bill's amazing expeditions and reading his explorer's tips on *How to Build a Raft*, *How to Live in a Volcano*, and even *How to Survive a Bear Attack*.

As Yuck and Little Eric were reading the

book, they heard the zipper of their tent opening. Polly poked her head through the entrance. "I've come to tell you that you're no longer allowed in our half of the yard," she said, then she marched off smugly.

Yuck and Little Eric looked out. Polly had laid Dad's garden hose down the middle of the lawn. On the other side of the yard, Lucy was putting up a sign that said NO EXPLORING ALLOWED.

Yuck turned to Little Eric. "This calls for special equipment," he said.

From the backpack Yuck took out his catapult, then he sneaked into the vegetable patch where Dad was planting seeds.

While Dad had his back turned, Yuck filled the catapult with handfuls of pumpkin seeds. He raced back to Little Eric and they lay by the hose, looking across at the enemy camp. They fired the seeds into the tree above Polly and Lucy's tent, then watched as birds flew to the branches to feed.

Inside their tent, Polly and Lucy were making daisy chains.

"What's that sound?" Lucy asked.

Polly listened. "It sounds like rain."

She poked her head out and saw bird poo plopping down from above. Their pretty tent was splattered with it. "Urgh! Poo!" she cried. A dollop of bird poo landed on Polly's head.

Lucy poked her head out and got plopped on too. "Eyugh! It's sticky!" she yelled, wiping her hair.

"Watch this," Little Eric whispered to Yuck. He ran to the flowerbed, where bees

were buzzing among the flowers. He picked a flower and took it to Lucy.

"Hey, you're not allowed on our side!" Lucy said.

"But I've come to give you this flower to say sorry," Little Eric told her.

"It's very pretty," Lucy said, surprised.

"It smells nice too. Sniff it."

Lucy put the flower to her nose.

BUZZZZ!

"Aaargh!" she yelled. A bee flew out. "A bee stung by dose!"

Lucy's nose was red and throbbing.

"Oh dear. That looks sore, Lucy," Little Eric said. "Perhaps you should go indoors."

Lucy pushed him back to the other side of the yard. "It's YOU who'll be going indoors. You'll see!"

All afternoon Polly and Lucy tried to get rid of Yuck and Little Eric, and Yuck and Little Eric tried to get rid of Polly and Lucy.

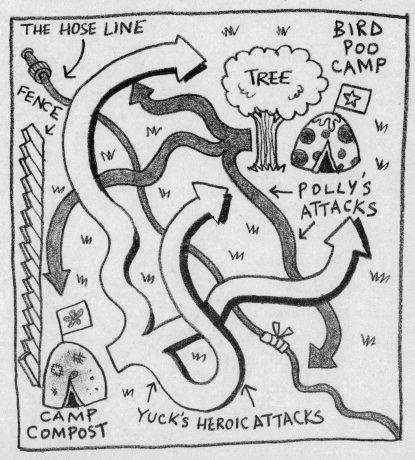

When Yuck and Little Eric were pretending they were exploring a desert, Polly turned on the hose to make it rain.

When Polly and Lucy were sunbathing, Little Eric swapped their suntan lotion for mayonnaise.

When Yuck and Little Eric were pretending they were climbing a mountain, Lucy pelted them with Dad's tomatoes.

And when Polly and Lucy were read-ing magazines in their tent, Yuck laid a trail of sugar to the entrance and a long line of ants scurried inside. Polly ran out screaming, "Help! There are ants in my pants!"

At about six o'clock, Mom called from the kitchen, "Dinner's ready." She came to the back door carrying a plate of hot dogs.

Yuck, Little Eric, Polly, and Lucy all rushed across the yard. Yuck and Little Eric scarfed down their hot dogs with lots of ketchup. They watched as Polly and Lucy put theirs onto paper plates to have as a picnic.

Yuck had a brilliant idea—a way to finally get Polly and Lucy to go back indoors. "Wouldn't it be scary if a big wild animal was to come and eat Polly and Lucy's food?" he whispered to Little Eric.

Quickly, Yuck ran to his
tent and fetched his fishing
rod from the pile of sur-
vival equipment. He'd made
it himself from a wooden
cane, a length of string, and
a bent pin. He sneaked across
the yard with Little Eric and
climbed the tree by Polly and
Lucy's tent.

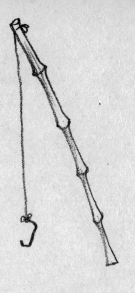

Yuck snapped two twigs from the tree and
handed them to Little Eric. "When Polly and
Lucy sit down, throw a twig into the bushes."

As Polly and Lucy sat on their blanket to
begin their picnic, Little Eric threw one of the
twigs into the
bushes. Polly
and Lucy
both looked
around.

"What was
that noise?"
Lucy asked.

Yuck lowered his fishing line. The bent pin hooked Polly's hot dog from the bun and he quickly pulled it up.

Polly turned back around. "Hey! Where's my hot dog?" she cried. She glared at Lucy. "Did you steal my hot dog?"

"It wasn't me," Lucy said.

Yuck and Little Eric giggled.

"Now," Yuck whispered again.

Little Eric threw the other twig into the bushes.

"Listen," Lucy said. "I heard it again. There's something moving in the bushes."

As Polly and Lucy looked around, Yuck lowered his fishing line again. The bent pin hooked Lucy's hot dog and he quickly pulled it back up.

"What if it was an animal?" Lucy said, turning back around. "Hey! My hot dog is gone too!" She glared at Polly. "Did you steal my hot dog?"

"It wasn't me," Polly said.

As Polly and Lucy started arguing, Yuck and Little Eric scarfed down the hot dogs, then climbed down from the tree.

"What's the matter with you two?" Yuck asked.

"Lucy stole my hot dog," Polly said.

"No. Polly stole MY hot dog," Lucy said.

"Maybe an animal ate them," Yuck said.

Polly and Lucy looked at Yuck, puzzled.

"An animal?" Lucy asked.

"What animal?" Polly asked.

"A WILD animal!" Yuck told them, glancing to the bushes.

"A really wild, hot-dog-eating animal," Little Eric added.

"It was probably something dangerous," Yuck said. "Like a bear!"

"A bear!" Lucy cried, glancing around nervously.

"Don't be silly," Polly said. "There aren't bears in the yard."

"I'd be careful if I were you," Yuck told them. "If a hungry bear's around here, then

it might come back tonight to eat YOU."

Lucy looked up at the sky. It was starting to get dark. "I don't want to be eaten by a bear," she whimpered.

Yuck and Little Eric strolled back to their tent giggling.

"Do you think they fell for it?" Little Eric whispered.

"If not, they soon will," Yuck replied.

As night fell, Yuck took a flashlight from his backpack and put on the Hairy-Bear Beast Glove. He crept to the flowerbed and made big paw prints in the mud as if a bear had been there.

Little Eric crept to the tree by Polly and Lucy's tent. While they were inside, he took a stick and scratched claw marks into the tree

trunk. Then Yuck and Little Eric hid in the bushes.

"*GRRRR*," Yuck said.

"*GRRRR*," Little Eric said.

In the tent, Polly and Lucy were opening

their midnight feast—a big bag of marshmallows.

"What's that noise?" Lucy asked. "It sounded
like an animal growling."

"It's probably just a squirrel," Polly said.

"But squirrels don't growl."

Polly unzipped the tent and shone her
flashlight outside.

"*GRRRR*," she heard from the bushes.

"I don't like this," Lucy said nervously.

Yuck and Little Eric quietly crawled behind the tree. Yuck stuffed the Hairy-Bear Beast Glove up his T-shirt, and they stepped out.

Polly shone her flashlight on them. "What are you two doing here?" she asked.

"We've come to warn you," Yuck replied. "We just saw a bear."

"Nonsense. There aren't bears in the yard."

"Yes, there are. We saw a big one sniffing around your tent."

"It was sharpening its claws on this tree," Little Eric said.

Polly pointed her flashlight at the tree and saw the claw marks on it.

"It tramped across the flower-bed," Yuck said.

Polly shone her flashlight on the flower-bed and saw the paw prints in the mud.

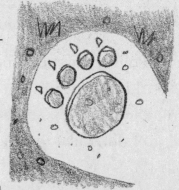

Lucy reached from the tent and tugged

on Polly's ankle. She was trembling. "Bears are dangerous, Polly," she said.

Polly looked at Yuck suspiciously. She shone her flashlight into his eyes, trying to see if he was lying. "If there's really a bear in the yard, how come you're not afraid?"

"Because we're explorers," Yuck told her. "Explorers aren't afraid of anything."

"You'd better not be up to something," Polly said, and she ducked back into the tent to find Lucy.

"I'm scared," Lucy said. "Let's go indoors."

"But it doesn't make sense," Polly told her, popping a marshmallow into her mouth. "Bears don't live in the yard. Yuck's just trying to scare us."

At that moment, something started scratching on the side of their tent.

"Listen!" Lucy whispered.

It sounded like claws.

"GRRRR . . . GRRRR," they heard.

"It's right outside," Lucy said. "It's coming to get us!"

They saw the tent's zipper moving upward. A clawed, hairy hand reached inside!

Then they heard a voice. "Get back, bear! Shoo!" it said. It sounded like Yuck.

Suddenly the clawed hand vanished and the growls stopped. The zipper on the tent opened and Yuck peered inside. "It's okay. I scared it off," he said.

Polly and Lucy were both trembling.

"You scared off a bear? How?" Polly asked.

"It was easy," Yuck replied. Tucked into his pants was his book *How to Survive in the Wild*. He pulled it out and showed it to them. "This book could save your life. It shows how to scare off a bear, how to wrestle a bear, and even how to trap a bear too. What a pity you haven't read it."

Yuck pointed at Polly and Lucy's bag of marshmallows. "The bear was probably after  those," he said. "You should give them to me to look after, then go indoors where it's safe."

Polly clutched the marshmallows tightly. "I'm not giving you these. These are our midnight feast."

"Well, don't blame me if the bear comes back," Yuck said. He zipped up the tent, then walked off giggling.

Polly and Lucy huddled together.

"I don't want to get eaten," Lucy said. "Please, can we go indoors?"

"Wait a second," Polly told her. "Look at this." She was shining her flashlight at a book by her side. It was Yuck's book. "He must have accidentally left it behind," she whispered. It was open on a page headed *How to Make a Bear Trap.*

There was a picture of a net with a rope attached to it. "I've got an idea," Polly said, sniggering. "If we can trap that bear, we could set it loose on Yuck and Little Eric!"

"That would get rid of them once and for all," Lucy said.

Polly unzipped the tent. "Come on."

"Where are you going?" Lucy asked.

"We need a net," Polly told her.

Under the cover of darkness, Polly and Lucy tiptoed to Yuck and Little Eric's tent. They could hear snoring.

"Yuck's got a net in his survival equipment," Polly whispered. She unzipped the tent and saw Yuck and Little Eric in their sleeping bags with their eyes closed. Their survival equipment was by Yuck's feet. Polly reached in and dragged out the net and rope.

"Nicely done," Lucy said, and they crept back across the yard to prepare the bear trap.

Yuck and Little Eric opened their eyes.

"They fell for it," Little Eric whispered.

"This is going to be fun." Yuck giggled.

Yuck and Little

Eric peered out of their tent and saw Lucy
shining a flashlight while Polly set up the
bear trap. They watched as Polly laid
the net on the ground by the tree
and attached the rope to it. She
threw the rope over a branch,
then dragged its end into her
tent. Lucy placed a hand-
ful of marshmallows on
the ground as bait,
then dashed inside
after Polly.

Yuck and Little Eric sneaked across the yard. They went indoors to find Mom.

"Hi, Mom," Yuck said.

"What's the matter? Can't you two sleep?" Mom asked.

"We're thirsty," Yuck told her. "Please, could we have a glass of milk?"

"Of course you can," Mom said. She took a carton of milk from the fridge and poured Yuck and Little Eric a glass each.

"Polly and Lucy would like some too," Yuck said.

"Can't they sleep either?"

"They asked if you'd take it out to them. They're tucked up in their sleeping bags."

Mom poured two more glasses of milk and carried them outside.

Polly and Lucy were huddled in their tent, clutching the end of the rope. "Listen," Polly whispered. "I can hear something."

Footsteps were coming across the yard.

"It's the bear," Lucy said excitedly.

"Get ready," Polly told her.

They both gripped the rope tightly.

The footsteps stopped outside the front of their tent.

"Now!" Polly said.

They both pulled hard on the rope. There was a *WHOOSH* as the net shot upward, then an "AARGH!"

"We've got it!" Polly said triumphantly. She leaped from the tent and shone her flashlight . . .

"M-M-Mom?"

Swinging in the net was Mom. She was covered with milk! "Polly! What on earth do you think you're doing?" she shrieked.

"I-I-I thought you were a bear," Polly said, surprised.

"A bear? Don't be ridiculous! Get me down from here this instant!"

Polly let go of the rope and the net dropped to the ground. Mom threw it off and stood up, wiping milk from her face. "Polly, Lucy, you're to come inside at once!" she said crossly.

"But, Mom—"

"That's the last time you two go camping in the yard!"

As Mom dragged Polly and Lucy toward the house, they passed Yuck and Little Eric running the other way.

Yuck was wearing the Hairy-Bear Beast Glove. He gave Polly a wave.

"It was you, Yuck!" Polly said angrily. "YOU were the bear! I HATE you!"

"GRRRR . . . Good night," Yuck said, giggling.

Little Eric ran to Polly and Lucy's tent and

picked up the marshmallows from the ground. "Look, Yuck! Food rations!" he called.

Yuck and Little Eric scarfed down the marshmallows, then both raised their hands, making the sign of THE CLAW.

"GRRRR. It's great to be in the wild!"

OTHER HILARIOUS
YUCK BOOKS

MATT AND DAVE

YUCK

YUCK'S AMAZING UNDERPANTS

MATT AND DAVE

YUCK

YUCK'S SLIME MONSTER

MATT AND DAVE

YUCK

YUCK'S FART CLUB

MATT AND DAVE

YUCK

YUCK'S PET WORM

MATT AND DAVE

YUCK

YUCK'S BIG BOOGER CHALLENGE